The Great Hot Air Balloon Adventure
Published by SDH
Copyright © Stephen D Holmes

First Edition 2016

A catalogue record for this book is available from the British Library.

978-1-5262-0412-7

Printed in England

Today like any other day, best friends Tom and Jessica finished school, walked up the steep hill, ran down the other side and back to their houses.

They rushed through their front doors, shouted "helloooooo!" to their Mummies, straight out of the back door, into the garden, through the hole in the fence and back together again to play catch.

At tea time, both Mummies yelled "diiinnnnnnneeeer!". Jessica and Tom skipped back and ate their tea, before having a bath ready for bed.

Every night, Jessica and Tom would peer out from their bedroom windows, watching
a magical hot air balloon gently sail across the sparkling starry sky.

eventually disappearing behind the full moon.
They would both yawn, wave goodnight and fall fast asleep in their cosy beds.

The following night, they watched the hot air balloon disappear behind the moon again.... but this time, something different happened....

It reappeared! Slowly moving back across the moonlit sky. Jessica and Tom gasped, it was now so near it was above their houses.

Then gently landed in the middle of Jessica's garden!

Tom ran straight downstairs, meeting Jessica by the hole in the fence. A rabbit, a very smartly dressed rabbit, wearing a top hat and tweed suit stepped out of the basket. "Good evening, I've noticed you watching my balloon every night. Would you like to go for an expedition?"

Tom was slightly nervous, but Jessica stepped forward eagerly "Yes please Mr Rabbit". "How exceedingly marvellous" replied the very well spoken Rabbit.

The balloon gently rose above the lawn, floating high above the houses and over the hills. "Where are we off to?" asked Tom. "Why, my little adventurers, we are off to the whitest, fluffiest cloud you can find".

The balloon swiftly landed on a cloud that looked like giant cotton wool. They jumped out and bounced. The cloud was like a giant trampoline! Jumping, giggling and somersaulting, they laughed so much they kept falling over.

"Brave Explorers! Time for refreshments". Mr Rabbit poured Jessica and Tom the creamiest hot chocolate they had ever seen. Glug, glug, glug. They gulped down their delicious drinks, leaving them with chocolate moustaches!

"Oooooooaaaaaaaaaa", yawned Tom. "Don't worry my intrepid trail blazers, I ask of you one more favour, then we shall head home". "Where are we off to next?" enquired an excited Jessica. "We are off to the enchanted forest, look out for the tallest tree".

The balloon continued on its way, soaring high
above lakes, hills and fields towards the forest.

"I see it! There's the tallest tree", shouted Tom. "Top notch tree spotting", replied Mr Rabbit. "Prepare to land!" The balloon touched down lightly on a large branch.

"At the end of the branch lives Mr Owl". Jessica and Tom stepped out of the basket, carefully walking towards a small wooden door.

"Knock, knock", the door opened. "Twit, twooo, how do you do", said the Owl. "Hello Mr Owl, here's your hot chocolate. "My, my, excellent, thank you", and with that Mr Owl quickly gulped down his hot chocolate, kissed goodbye to his wife and flew off into the night sky.

"Ooooooaaaaaaaaaaaaaa", now Jessica
let out a huge yawn. "Time to get you home
adventurers", Mr Rabbit pulled on the cord and
the balloon once again set sail.

Back over the lakes, forests and fields, until they reached Jessica's garden.

"Much obliged for your marvellous work", Mr Rabbit tipped his top hat. "I trust you had a most wonderful time". "We did, thank you", replied Jessica and Tom. Waving goodbye, the balloon set off high into the night sky.

Tom and Jessica crept back upstairs to their bedrooms and gazed out of their windows, watching the balloon float across the glittering stars and beyond the moon.

Little did they know, every night following their magical adventure, Mr Owl would check on Jessica and Tom, before flying back to the enchanted forest to let Mr Rabbit know they were both safely tucked up in bed and fast asleep.